SUCCUBUS ARTS

MINI-BOOKS BY THE AUTHOR

The Abandoned and The Undead.
Breast Clamps
Dramatic Theme Swells.
Furball A poetry zine written completely in Anglo-Saxon runes.
Kettle Memento Mori.
Nymph
Odin's Legislations.
Platinum Blondage.
Poems, Prayers, and Curses.
A Taazhpuur Grammar & Lexicon.
A Taazhpuur-English Dictionary.
Towards a More Respectful Language: The Need for a Neutral Third Person Pronoun.
The Book of Mark. A Gothic & English Interlinear Edition.

SUCCUBUS ARTS

Philosophic incantations in verse on love & lust & undying passion.

Gregory Scaff

SUCCUBUS MEDIA

ISBN 978-0-9970129-0-3

@gregoryscaff on Twitter

Succubus Arts—Gregory Scaff on Facebook

SuccubusMedia on YouTube;
https://www.youtube.com/watch?v=DXbs8Pb5rvU

Gratitude to Mazy Kyst for the nymph tableau
vivant cover art.
.
This is a SuccubusMedia Book.

ADVANCE PRAISE

"With inventive wordplay, a twinkling eye posed on our sacred and profane humanity, Scaff's erotic poetry is more than the sum of its pleasing parts. Like the great roman comic dramatist Terence, nothing human is alien in our shared perversity, mundanity, and grandeur. Le mot juste is Gregory's flair, and doggerel hides a dogged seriousness. There's pleasure and darkness in his Satyricon. Enjoy him."
James MacGregor Byrne;
Critic, Cad, Crank, & Curmudgeon

"Because of our Spiral Staircase Readings, I cannot help but read Gregory Scaff's work in his voice and cadence. His erotic poetry is therefore unsettlingly delightful for me. I invite you to read "Succubus Arts" with a cauldron of strangers, whether in your mind or in person."
Theodore DeGraff
CARPAZINE

"Scaff takes one into a world both sensuous and voluptuous with his poems of unabashed carnality, he makes no apology for making one a voyeur into his imagination."
Ginger Lambert
Instagram handle:
Steampunkibyginger

"Of all the next-level poets I have had the honor to know and spend time with, Gregory Scaff has a way of crafting his work that makes me want to dissect him to see what's in there. That's gross. Sorry."
Rocky Jones
Evil Grin Poetry Series

DEDICATION

Qenaï meinaï þïzaï lïuboston ad lusta.

To the love of my life, the blindingly sparkly Muffin. This book would not be without you.

ACKNOWLEDGEMENTS

Thank you to Professor G. Pagliorulo, & to
Rocky, Ginger, Mazy, Theodore, Nyla, & to James.
My debt to others is too high to repay.

"Modesty is a crime; Shamelessness is a Virtue. I am the Whorax, I speak for the Sluts."
Mazy Kyst

THE SUM OF WE

Enraptured I enwomb you—
ravenous for the incandescent
pumping bliss of you within me.

With every mystic, amaranthine taste
our skin flames—our atoms
supernova, and you and
I and all Existence fades in
waves of flickering white, and
I am you, and I and
I am white flashing light,
and we are
Infinity.

ON ROUND WORLD IN THE ROUND DIMENSION

Within the barbed wire of
Triangular ghetto
the lone Rectangle
crept shyly up to
the one Square—
dry mouthed and with
chocolates—
but reaped a blistering of
"piss off you sicko!
I stick to my own kind."

Birds when first pushed
inherit an emerald and sparkly gift-
like hot sex they
zoom light years to
rip the veils between
Pasteur and Galileo.
what an emerald and sparkly gift.

FOR THE SAKE OF PIXIE WINGS

"Who would give a law to lovers?
Love is unto itself a higher law."
Boethius

I will not howl in languid misery,
I'll wail no dirges, no agonized laments,
no litany of searing anguish.
But, if you die first I won't relent, if
you die first I will not let go.
I will discern the right time–
the right quarter of the
moon, the right day, the right
second, I'll burn
the right candle, dance the right
dance. I'll stain your marmoreal name
with rendered vulture's fat and torrid rum,
I'll bleed black the grass with
a slaughtered goat or throat slit
dog, I'll beg to the right
gods, chant the right spells.
I'll feed the earth from
my own sorrow-dark veins until the
tenacious mud retches you
up, until you crawl from
your grave still
cobwebbed in the velvet amethyst
of our wedding, and when
you rise our eternal passion will

shine like moon-buffed pixie wings–
if, that is, and only if
you promise, not to
snack upon my living brains.

ON THE HIGHER SIDE OF FELICITY

Drawn to the lines of my ass and the
glittering spikes on my jacket the balding
pinstripe at the Harvard T wandered over
to humbly ask me for a date.

His apartment was a den of mahogany and
marble inquisitionally replete with a cedar
trunk by the bed delightfully filled to the lid
with chains and black accessories.

Kneeling naked and whimpering, the
man begged for both severity and
moderation, he was of two minds, and
his lower leapt when I stepped out of my
jeans and strutted over, where like a
good puppy he gratefully licked the spit
off my Docs. I shackled him to the
bedposts, all tenderly clamped and gagged,
then raked his flanks and squished his grapes,
I mapped his thrashing body with a
whip until his ass glowed like Rudolph's
nose and his muffled screams ricocheted like
bullets.

I flogged his weenie holding it still and
stiff and tight in my fishnet grip, pounding
it with a crop like a punk rock drummer
watching him buck with each swat, howling

non-stop for mercy, so I-ever-so-slowly-
and-from-up-close doused the swollen tip of
his cock in rivulets of flaming wax until he
gushed luminous strands of pearl.

Leaving the man chained, butt-up and crying,
I ransacked his fridge to dine on smoked eel
and French bread, while guzzling thick
Austrian wine and watching VH1 on a wide
screen.

Such hard work for a hundred bucks.

SEE YOU

After New Orleans–
after everything,
when cyanotic
becomes you,
when the stain of
tears has faded and
the night roses tatter,
then I shall own
you – oh you of the burnt
bone eyes–right off
the block I shall claim
you as mine for my own
exquisite, everlasting play.

Even now rapturous devil
girls line up slavering to
chain you, to spread you
between the icy marble columns
of my grotto, of my hermetic
cavern carved of demon
tusks and carpeted with virgin's
cunts. There I shall be your
eternal, infernal Grand Inquisitor,
complete with the finest
instruments of my art– with
racks and wheels and iron
maidens, with whips
and clamps and assorted
probing tools. There in my dark

shrine of transcendent pain,
studded shackles tentacle like
mangrove webs across the onyx
ivory walls, deep below the
corrosive seas of the Chasm's
infinite, boiling flame.

Each dawn you will
guzzle succubus milk
straight from the nipple, to
awaken eager, whole, and
unsliced like Odin's warriors
from our long,
long nights of play.
I will carve away your secrets
from your tender and lacerated
flesh, I will peel away your masks,
we have Eternity–
because MY Goddess is
a loving Goddess–she will
bless me–and you–you
will be a Houri in your
Paradise.
Isn't this romantic?

See
you
in
Hel.

CHASSOHOWITZKA GIFT
Gratitude to Mazy Kyst for
the nymph tableau vivant.

Shrouded in the moist mossy night
of an evergreen veil I stared Argus-
eyed at a jade-haired forest girl haloed
in sun-gold, birdsong and emerald—
glitter-clad in rapture–buffing herself
lustrous upon an altar of clover.

The pearled-rose oak sprite plucked
with butterfly whispers at the diamond
tips of her bunny breasts–her Botticelli
curls sunflowered and rippled–her pine-
bough eyes cuddled blindly in a radiant and
fallopial trance while an ever louder
stampede of moans escaped the soft
corral of her coral lips.

Windlessly sparking to life, my pine
night and the encircling dangle of
Spanish moss hurricane danced to the
raging samba of the nymph's glistening
fingers, feverishly polishing her hot
fuchsia orchid.

The faster her hands reverberated,
the higher the dryad's thighs shivered –
arcing repeatedly in burnished rivulets,
her hips pumped like a hammer's

knock until she'd attained a fiery
incandescent tranquility—then, curling
from the crystal sand, an oak tendril
spiraled between her knees as the
lynx-eared wood nymph glimmered and
smiled away into sunbeam.

Sliding over the river a frigate
bird billowed out its scarlet throat.
Marsh rabbits rustled through
lime sparkling palmetto fronds–
what a pleasant day for a canoe ride

GROUND ZERO SORBET

Baudelaire and Lovecraft,
Stephen Jay Gould and Vampirella.
Frazetta, not Picasso.
You quoted Catullus at the bar.

My salty cosmopolite, you were
an atmospheric glow of elven
eyes in a throbbing darkened room,
you were a feral horse-mane–
you were Docs and a Siouxsie-armored
porcupine jacket–a lace-bra
gift in fishnet and French
thong panties. You were zaftig's
quintessence dipped in satin milk.

On the bed you blended
with the strawberry
sorbet I licked
off your vulva.

FLESHECSTACY

Last night's phone call
tasted like gossamer;
I demand the full meal;
you alone will gratify.

How can I avoid peppering you
with kisses? Gnawing at your throat
like a famished vampire,
you of the silk velvet skin and
sable scintillant hair? You are an
Absolute – Beauty's very Ideal.
The gluteal arches of your
smile are Resurrection—how could
artists paint any other flower?

Dripping and pulsating, hunger-
swooning in delirium, I tongue-tickle
a banquet trail over and around the
phosphorescent apples of your breasts,
nibbling at the gloried halo of
each nuclear cherry—discovering
like Atlantis the satin chalice of
your navel, the porcelain swellings
of your glassine hips.

Glued passionately to your mammary
curves, the slim shine of your calves
telephones—it e-mails—it faxes.

I whisper kiss the kitten skin of that
lustery beacon, up to the rosy nexus,
the craving Valentine of your juicy
welcome, nestled timidly, like a ten
pound ruby. Moaning, your delectable
thighs grip me in the undulating hothouse
warmth of left and right.
Kissing the crest of your petals I
serenade you, deeper and deeper,
while our coupled hearts hammer a
surround sound staccato of ragged
breathing and raspy urgings.

Again and again, like an unbroken
horse, your hips buck skyward before
I untie you.

SILVER LININGS

First poor Ophelia got that
horrible fortune
cookie which said "you
are a joy to all you meet."

Then, my moonrise
horoscope–which seems
awfully harsh but does
add a silver lining–told me,

"Hail hail
fire and bale.

From the sulfured grave
black Hell will break
the bath of flame
will not abate
devil wings define
your Fate.

The black Abyss shall
screeching rise
avernal claws will
claim the skies
at eleven fifty-nine
tonight.

Ruby-eyed and howling the
Reaper shall smash his

chains, He shall
cinder his Books of Names,
swinging His sickle freely
till human skulls pile up like
skyscrapers, and there atop
those ivory ziggurats saber-
fanged demons will offer
wailing hearts to their fierce
God–then never shall the
succubi and incubi of night
time longings ever
rest."

ZEUS' DAUGHTER

I met her strolling on Clearwater beach
She asked me out for coffee
One look in her eyes—ohhhh
The goddess Aphrodite
Came home with me last night

Pizza and wine and kisses

She left before I woke up
No note
No last name
No address

She claimed to be an
Anthropology major at U.S.F.
But I'm not stupid—someone so
Agonizingly gorgeous
Can't be human

Beauty sears, it chars, it hurts
To look upon her scorched
Like an inferno, like
Mount Vesuvius,
A no-man's land of
Grateful intoxication.

READY-MADE POEM: DRYER

Insert coins.

Push–
slide in, and
slowly pull out.
Repeat for more time.
Push red button to start.
Cool down, air only.

WHITE SLACKS AT THE DRIVE-IN

Blonde mane, tight white jeans,
Mutinous butt bursting free,
Dreams are made of you.

--Three lines from Bedrock, an innocence
Ago; a syllabic cudgel,
Elephantine, littoral—perhaps.

Who knows the movie, the night's a void,
Just that smile—the twin of my future love—
those glam locks & those delicious bubbles.
Cinéma verité strikes whimsical,
Like faerie dust.

Yes, a veneer, & the rest is vacuum,
A whiff of a memory of a glimpse.
Each day's tedium demands Beauty,
Beauty sears my helixes,
I drip gratitude, & no regrets.

Oh, sweet mystery of life,
Gloria in excelsis deo.
Dreams are still made of you.

WINDING LANE APARTMENTS
Clearwater, Florida c. 1983

A radio wall blasted the Bee
Gees from the second floor.

In the parking lot we stared up
at the woman fucking
on a tabletop by the window
the growing line of naked men
around her—they were back lit
in a blinding light & displayed
by funky orange curtains
spread wider than the
woman's thighs.

Howling she looked radiant,
triumphant.

I envisioned enduring
that piercing music
to stand in that joyous line
of ecdysiast givers
then when that moment
of glory arrived
when I'd receive access to
that silky frame
I would join the mystics in ecstasy.

Instead I stood in

the parking lot
two nights in a row
by the third she'd been evicted
opportunity knocks then runs away.

AN ADOLESCENT REVERIE- OR- HAROLD WIGGINS MEETS BETTIE PAGE

Dancing in Vienna,
holding close against the
pliant sway of Bettie's liquid
bosoms, the breathy
escalation of her
cushioned flanks, Harold gazed
into her empyreal eyes,
he peppered the ebony
velvet of her hand with kisses–
ardently declaring,

"oh Mon Cheri, we are fated
together, you and I, my darling,
my pet, my soul mate. We'll dine
in Rome and dance in Paris,
we'll ignite the world
with our passion."

Then a clinking glass gashed
the air. Harold's family stared
at him like meercats from around
the table.

His little sister whined,
"hurry up Harold!   We're all
ready for the chocolate cake,
while you're still gnawing on

that drumstick!"

Harold's father mumbled,
"after supper, you and I should
have a little talk."

Nodding, Harold studied
his peas and mashed potatoes,
remembering the silk of dark
hair upon his cheek.

VIDEO MUSIC AWARDS

"I used to go to clubs in crazier outfits"
Rose McGowan

Dear US magazine,
Regarding your October
Sixth, 2003 issue;

So what if Rose McGowan
Wore a see-through,
Chain mail apron and
Matching thong to MTV's
Video Music awards?

Your Fashion Police
Ranked her among the
Worst Dressed because
Of that outfit;

Rose McGowan is a
Creative and multi-
Talented actor who
Does not need to be
Suppressed by your
Flatulate and dated,
Drama queen
Hyper-criticism.

For Humanity's sake,

Let the woman wear
What she wants,
Even if it is just
Chain; especially,
If it is just chain.

DEAR PLAYBOY

Dear Playboy,
I have been a
Fan of Charisma
Carpenter's for
Many years and was
Ecstatic to see her
On your June cover.

I have always loved
your magazine, but
Imagine my
Horror when I
Opened it and, in
An otherwise
Gorgeous pictorial,
Saw that you
Had squinched us all
On the booty shots!!!

OMGZ!!!
HOW COULD
YOU PLAYBOY!!!
And with bootylicious
Charisma Carpenter!
Please, she deserves
Another pictorial.
Hey to Hef.
Sincerely, Gregory

NYMPHOLEPTIC
TRANSFIGURATIONS

Helen, you've returned from
Attica, radiant in a knotted
tangle of whirled sunbeam,
a valiant band-aid top
courtly in its vain efforts
to stem that cascade,
floral flip-flops, dark
reflecto-glasses, and
tightly furrowed crimson
short-shorts embroidering a
magnificent Hagia
Sophia derriere – Lady

Liberty in truth, oiled in
coconut, a fourth of July
super-nova, distilled Delirium
wheeling a shopping cart.

My ceiling crowds like
oil-stained gravel and
the copralitic phone sheds
vacuous chimes of perpetual
grief.

Until that afternoon
life's long corrosion
scraped over and again

like the bitter dusts of
breakfast, but remembering
you my cherished eternal
ghost, I am chocolate &
sunflowers.

BRING YOUR OWN

A new smelling beamer off
the lot and coffins of
murdered flowers!
To hell with you and
your pretentious bribes—
everyone knows salvation
is in the details.

After dating Mr. Self
Absorbed Grand Poo-Bah
this SWF seeks a white
knight Mr. Maybe—
a sensitive someone who
will love me sweetly
who will love me truly
who will love me deeply—
with bonbons and boxes
and boxes of condoms.

COCONUT AND SALT WAVES

"Solitude and isolation are painful beyond human
endurance."
Jules Verne

The south wind sang in rustling
leaves under a lazy sun and
I could almost hear the lapping
of the waves of Tahiti the swish
of grass skirts the thump of golden
feet on satin sand

I imagine that the mate of my
soul is not local—that
perfumed in coconut and salt waves
naked she walks on white sand
between emerald leaves
under a parrot filled lemon sky

night-haired and extra-mammalian
her dark eyes betray a deep reflective
IQ crowned in crimson petals

yet with Gaia's over-many my total
mate is probably a centenarian bag lady
dying in the alleyways of Ulan Bator
or Calcutta—

even now someone
is stealing her shopping cart while

another yank's off my beloved's shoes

she may not return again
until long after my death
solitude and celibacy and
I are good friends.

DREAMWORLD

You asked what dream world I live in;
mine is a more sparkly realm than
yours—it's a crowded, white-hot
diamond beach replete with swaying
palms and salty breezes.

Everyone there is naked; it's the law.
I am the sole, official, Suntan
Inspector and Lotion Applicator; also
the only man.

I offer vibra-therapy to the medically needy,
I carry every flavor of lotion as well,
to ensure the desired tan, to guarantee
that no one's precious tenders burn.

One of the Swedish Bikini Team struts by;
she requires obvious medical attention. Astrid
stands while I caress her breasts, her legs,
her biceps—I inspect her every exquisite
inch, I knead her poor, overworked gluteals,
oiling her all over.

But wait—she is in crisis,
she's been training, she suffers from muscular
cramps. I must prevent her from drowning!

Laying her down, I apply a purely medicinal,
pulsating device directly to the hood,

holding it there until her thrashing ends, thus
freeing her of danger.

Afterwards the entire team lines up for
treatment, legs wide, breasts and pubic
mounds shiny and eager. All of them
need tanning cream, all of them complain
of muscle cramps, the poor, poor, dears;
their volleyball has been intense.

Harsh life on Daydream beach.

Here in your bitter, Prozac reality,
we're driving on north 89 toward
the land of Holsteins and decrepit
barns.

A grubby green semi from
West Bridgewater, Massachusetts,
blocks us in on the left. Scarred
ashen cliffs coffin us in upon the

right. Our wheels slip over grungy
snow, the dingy vomit from an
angry, ashtray sky. Buckle up under
eighteen, New Hampshire, it's the law.

BREATHTAKING

In my wet dream, you lay,
sprawled naked under
the loving gaze of an
idle sun, upon a thick
mattress of mammoth
fur, which covered an
enormous slab of a high
stone altar, surrounded
by the far-flung sky and
the pink marble ruins
of a temple hallowed by
Aphrodite.

Not sparing an inch,
you mapped your naked
flesh, reading your body
in Braille with feather
kisses, your blonde skin
gleaming in the Grecian
sun, fingers franticly
stroking the rocket-tips
of your delicate breasts,
the translucent satin of
your hips, the urgent
glistening of your rosy
petals, until your moaning
stopped and your back
arched, when your burning
face blushed, your gorgeous

eyes spiraled tight, and your
velvet lips pulled wide in
a drawn out, silent howl.

Then you lay still, crowned
by the lustrous sun like
a living image of Venus.

Those cheekbones,
those eyes, that nose,
that smile.

RUMORS IN THE GOOD OLE' USA

Nourished at the organic store
on Old Faithful
rumors
of Dionysian sex,

deprived
lost skeletons
belly crawl
through grit and
cacti,
only to find

a drip of water
on
damp
sand.

SEEING YOU

I hate the fact
that I love
to watch you move,
that it intoxicates me
to watch the oscillating
jiggle of your naked flesh.

When you walk or run,
naked in stride,
your flexuous body,
your striving thighs,
and glorious gluteals,
all sing of joy.

I'm in rapture to
view your
deep cornflower
eyes, your decadently
flaming pillow lips,
I thrill to see your
coral-tipped breasts
quiver and sway,
to see your white
throat glow translucent,
to see the ripple of
the muscles of your back.

I love to watch
you move, you are

stunning when you
lift a glass and your
biceps bulge, and
asleep, your silky,
vespine stomach
takes my breath away.

I hate that you
don't like being
naked or being admired,
or that you think you
are fat and ugly,
and that I have to
pay to watch someone
else be naked.

HYPNOPOMPIC WET DREAM

Hiking beyond the complex parking lot,
I wandered onto a hidden, frond-veiled trail
between scruffy pines that wound along a
lime-velvet alligator pond that squawked with
Muscovy ducks, through a coral snake forest
of serrated palmetto, to discover at the end,
the vaunted apartment spa and laundry shed
in a gold-bright glade of hot sand and sun-lust.

The shed was a desolate cell of concrete
bristling with cockroaches, a little-used
closet which housed a 40 watt bulb and
a rusted washer/dryer made famous
on brochures as "The Laundromat" by
charlatan realtors. Scant feet away,
nestled in an areola of sandspurs,
the secluded Jacuzzi was an awkward
affair of insolent jets and gritty
water, often drained and shut off, barren
and deserted even in daylight.

With three jobs and ninety plus hours of
cinder-block labor a week, I was under-
fed and over-sore, alone each night far
from the distant clump of apartments,
pursuing welcome nirvana in the
affectionate swirls of the whirlpool,
soaking away my pains until the

temptress edge of sleep dragged me home.

One night in the small hours, alone and
desperate for even a faint sense of
life and unrestraint, alert for the protests
of startled ducks, I dared to strip, gripping
my shorts warily by moon light. But then—
as the ample moon's unspanked ass
sailed on by—I succumbed to tranquility
and cannon-balled into a tropical
dream world, where I drifted on the cobwebbed
heartbeat of the sun-glimmering sea.
Polished ivory naiads grappled passionately
with their shark-skinned triton lovers,
surrounding me in a scaly carnal rodeo
of silken breasts and triple-cocks. I saw
kissing, and I saw claw-marks; some
embraced, languidly undulating in a caressing,
fantail tangle; others ravished and bit, grabbing
hair and wrenching arms in a brawling,
copulatory free-for-all. Their collective orgasmic
thrashings lashed the eager surf itself to crest
and froth, and I in my slumbered faerie realm
nestled on the foamy breasts of this swelling flood.

I was balanced in the flickering doorway
between delirium and awakening,
gazing up at you, O lion-maned
Aphrodite; you stood all naked and
bouncy on the labial sands of Paphos.
Your supple legs rippled and glowed like honey
as you cordially sprawled them apart.
A fierce, agonizing burning pulsed from

the base of my groin throughout the ends of
my being; I ached to embrace you, to
lose myself in the yielding satin of
your arms, to slither between the feathery
petals of your radiant pink orchid.

Then your eyes, glittering like faerie fire,
locked onto my crotch, and you smiled as bright
as marigolds. Rocking on volcanic
waves of desire, I looked down at the
throbbing turquoise veins of my erect cock;
it was a flag-pole swaying in the sea.

As if in slow motion, I watched myself
spurt again and again like Moby Dick;
My cock was a wanton marble fountain
spraying luminous strands of milky lust into
the wide and slutty air.

Then my eyes blinked open; I saw that I floated
out, unclothed, and gooey upon the cum-
spattered froth of the spa, and you, the tangible,
vanilla-scented succubus of my soul,

you stood over me, leaning in to scrutinize
my still pulsing cock. Unruffled, you hugged
a basket of stacked clothing to your abundant
hip while chatting casually but loudly
about detergents and colors and rinses
to someone else inside the Laundromat.

I stared at you; my brain was a glacier
of frozen syrup. Your glam-rock mane hovered

in golden swirls like a giant, wavy
halo; your neon zebra half shirt and
your high cut wraparounds were mere whispers
of curvy gossamer, and your legs—your
legs gleamed like the sun. Floundering for my
shorts, I gaped at those Olympian legs,
those shining, beguiling, amber legs,
as you turned, walking away, saying good-
night to your friend.

COME OUT COME OUT

Every blastocyst a female,
Every male of us a trans.

Gender worries are carbon-dated, transcend.
Gender & its cravings dwell in
Chemistry & not the loins;
Multiplicity reigns; no one is a Xerox.
I believe in Klein's Grid, in Kinsey's seven-
Points & the gorgeous variations therein,

I believe in bones & blood & skin & flesh,
I believe in the apposites of male & female, &
The varieties in between; in the five sexes,
In the girls who wake up one day as boys,
In the many inter ones with this & that;
I believe in discordant trans, in the breadth
Of ones too plentiful & amazing to name,
You can pee next to me.

The motherly voice of Multiplicity
Calls out to you all,
Come out come out
Whoever you are.

NYLA

Hungrily my cock
laps the hallowed depths of you—
my siren craving.

Freya's arrived—
bow down O nymphs and dryads,
bow down.

Sacramentia!
Veneria!
Vagina!
Amoria!
Fallopia!
For a hallowed rite of rapture
I invoke you all.

If I could by chant of full moon spell
but shrink to Lilliputian—or
if you could merely look Godzilla eye-to-eye—
then I would salmon
through your coral gates to
sail your harlot seas,
emerging once more with the
flooding of your fountain tide—
my Second Coming.

Go back to Attica, Helen—
you mortal—you've

been upstaged.
Fade away into dreamland,
you water nymphs and pine-haired dryads;
all your wiggling is wasted, for
I have found my Ultima Thule.

I GAVE IT MY ALL

Matjam jah drigkam, unte du maurgina gaswiltam.
I Kor. 15:32

Where the lips of the sky French kissed the sea,
the gleaming mirror of the Gulf mingled into star-
shine.

It was a summer weekday, 1979.
I was eighteen, bronzed in flip-flops
& cut offs, racing dolphins in my kayak
across Saint Joseph Sound.

I stashed my Folbot at the nipple tip
of Caladesi's north.
Hot sand, white quartz,
Seagulls, sea oats & Spanish bayonet.

Two boats in three miles,
almost no one on the island, no ferry.

At the marina, stub-tailed raccoons raided garbage
cans.
The metal lids slammed down like dumpster gongs.

Alone, I picnicked past the empty docks,
by the tower in the rustling scrub.
Afterwards I hiked the nature trail
to the promoted scenic pond.

Towards the deepest part of the woods,
I thought, I am alone, all alone; daring,
I slipped off my shorts.
Naked in sun beams, tall pines,
& palmettoes, I skipped, I pirouetted,
I rhapsodically sang thunderous arias.
Naked teen in the woods.

I came upon a bench by a live oak;
a pair of women's brown sandals,
a pack of Camels & a lighter on the bench.
Odd, but ok, people forget things all the time.

There was an overshadowing branch.
I wanted to know scaling a tree naked.
I shucked my flip-flops, climbing
rapidly up the knots of the trunk,
scrambling out over the overhang.
I asked out loud, & the tree was cool,
I said, thank you tree.

As I straddled that branch, I felt a
desperate & dire need; a stiffness
blossomed without touch.
I handled my purple drive shaft,
My need wanted it fifteen feet up.

Because why not? I was alone.
I rubbed my bulbous knob lightly
against the granite rough of the bark,
against the smooth velvet of leaves.
My bruised cock swelled;
it's tissue skin ached terribly.

I delicately stroked my penile
slit with leaf stems, stickiness trickled out.
I hugged the arching tree branch,
rubbing myself upon it, I humped the
thick branch ever so slowly,
raspy breathing, moaning.

I caressed myself on top of the
branch, I caressed myself on this side,
& then on that side, & then, hanging
perilously, against the underside.

Sitting upright, I locked my
feet beneath the branch.
A shoot jutted from a knobby bump.
I inserted it, riding the knot cowgirl,
then reverse.
I spared nothing in touching myself.

Bouncing up & down tree fucking,
I polished my pre-cum cockhead;
I was frenzied, franticly stroking,
sweat-shiny, I struggled madly,
wrestling for an agonizing time.
The desired 'gasm shied away;
my porn-star gymnastics proved
arduous while trying not to fall.

Finally, I attained the glimmering;
My back arched, my feet cramped,
My ass flexed, my muscles clenched.
My eyes were blind pearls,
Shuddering, I howled my passion

loudly & without shame.
My creamy stream shot twenty feet,
I was a rock star.

Time had compressed; it had been over an hour.
Naked in emotion as in fact, I dressed
& continued my hike to the oaken stand.
Numinous above, numinous below.
A leaf-tannin pond circled by
a grove of gnarly primeval trees.
Cormorants, forest song & osprey calls,
swamp bunnies & armadillos in the brush,
all was magnificent with the world.

After awhile, begrudgingly I turned back.
Pine-drunk on a glorious day, I slogged off
trail, stomping raucously through
the whispering palms to scare off snakes.

In due course, I resumed the path;
ambling along, I came upon a
twenty-something couple next to the tree.
He stared at me, slack jawed, saying nothing,
holding a cigarette.
She sat on that bench, a bikini blonde
wearing the brown sandals.
Trying to be polite, I said,
"Sorry for making so much noise,
I didn't see you."

Smiling, her entire face blushed
a vibrant red, she replied,
"We didn't see you either."

A THREE-PART ANTHROPOLOGICAL TREATISE ON HUMAN DESIRES

Of Neandertals, Zana, & Polynesians.

I.

Many, many, befores before, back when
We were all tall, dark & Aurignacian,
We encountered those cavern trolls, those
Stubby-legged & brow-ridge people.
What clownish hair!
What fish belly skin!
What outlandish schnozzes!
They did not even roast marshmallows!

But we ignored all that, we ignored all that,
Because we peeked beneath
Their mammoth-fur loincloths,
& that we could not ignore;
We watched them deadlift
Buffaloes, & that we could not ignore.
We said, "Hey baby, step into
My tent," & they said
"I'm gonna climb you like a tree."

(These are my parents, & yours.)

II.

In 1850 Zana the ferocious wild
Woman with tremendous bazooms
Was dragged from the woods of southern Russia.
Though she fought & howled & bit, they locked her
In a cage for three years, from where the
Denigrations flew like explosive
Yersinia bumps.

Zana the ape-chick rips off all of her clothes!
Zana climbs trees like a monkey!
She is hairy as a chimp!
Zana sleeps in a hole in the ground!
She runs naked in the snow!
She can out-race horses!
Zana can carry 200 lbs.!
One handed!
Uphill!
Zana growled & grunted, but like Philomela,
Never said a word, alas.
Zana was "dirty," "ugly," "ape-like," "repellant."
Zana was not human; they branded her
a "yeti, a relic Neandertal, the Missing Link;"
Yet, & yet, Zana the ferocious ape-chick
Dropped a litter of Homo sapiens sapiens,
Which she caught when she was passed out drunk.

III.

Like those bigoted Captain Cooks who wrote
In their logs, "The natives are gruesome

In every respect, they are black & hideous,
With squished noses & bizarre appearance.
The crew has grown defiant & well nigh
Mutinous; despite threats of flogging &
Keelhauling, they continue to pull nails
From the ribs of the ship itself, in order
To pay the savages to fornicate
With them*."

*attribution unknown

YOUR VERY LIPS MANIFESTO

"The curves of your hip are like jewels, the work of
the hands of an artist..."
Song of Solomon

I

Wind wraith sky shatter,
star anvil clatter– luscious
your lips unself me.

Joyful you— delightful,
delectable, exhilarating!
Your liquid swayings,
those flying Romanesques!
The hypnotic ripples of
your sacred triple angles
stun me into ecstasy.

II

Bulletproof in your beach
towel, you scrunch the six
steps from the dressing room
to the pool so no one scopes
out the searing glory of you,
promenading in wispy,
Brazilian Lycra.

You cry that this is crinkled
and that is frizzled— that
these are fat but those are thin,
while this— this is just weird;
yet astonished passersby gape
after you, awakened by their
shamelessness into epiphany.

III

I want to kiss your blistering
pavement Highway 19;
you 98-degree sunstroking
cloud of exhaust,
I embrace you, for along
your route hallowed Splendor
shines like Selene
in thong clad Helens from
Fairy Land, who vend
from carts that gild your
path like sparklers beneath
a diamond and cottontail sky.

How sleek and glistening you
marketeers are, with your
legs gleaming like ivory tusks,
dizzying with those amber
fields of flesh, more
gorgeous than every sunset,
more spectacular than
the Milky Way—

so persist in your coy
wiggling, oh Florida nymphs,
drown me in pulchritude—
drench me in flesh,
in the beneficence of muscle
and skin and anatomical
veracity— plunge me in
the steamy flamingo
glow of bliss,
rocket me into Elysium

For you I am Kong howling
Atop the Empire State,

I can never devour my fill.

LUST-LETTERS TO OUR SELVES IN SEVERAL ANATOMICALLY INTERWOVEN PARTS, BECAUSE THE CONNECTION OF OUR PARTS CAUSES EARTH-SHATTERING KABOOMS

I am not afraid to say it,
O dear externals, how I love you!
O dreamy grottos! O sweet cylinders! O rampant
spheroids!
O toenails, O sacral Trinitarian lines, O calvarium!
In dumbfounded humility,
You are awesomeness distilled—you are
astronomic;
We are delicious.

The prizewinning tulips of my love are
Sennacherib's terraced & love-letter gardens of
Nineveh, where airport marshallers deify my
Illuminati pearl with vigilant intensity unto lush
overflowing, all the while raving litanies in the
syntax of centaurs to the Wonderland of my
Holland Tunnel & I tremble, thinking of you,
winged on the Technicolor rapture of my flamingo
calla lily.

The satyr rod of my love is an unchained piston, the
high obelisk of Great Zimbabwe looming over the
vast & empty steppes, where those shaven, off-

limits nomads whose herds of stiff-maned ponies
are as aphids to the gods, offer fragrant wineskins
of airag upon rocky cairns in my honor & I swoon,
thinking of you, grokking the silken granite of my
spire.

Bioluminescent, we flicker like silver lame'
Pixie dust in the noon cheery sun.

I & I,
I
am
Infinity.

ABOUT THE AUTHOR

Gregory Scaff describes himself as an out-of-place artifact; he is a 2D artist, a bibliophilic punk rock Dada poet who frequents Mid-Atlantic poetry readings,

Gregory holds a BA in Anthropology from USF. He is a longtime supporter for a sex positive culture.

Gregory's poetry has been published in Obelisk Magazine, Circle Works, The Valley Literary Magazine, New Reality Magazine, in Aequinox IV, Carpazine, & in Rat's Ass Review. He also self-prints DIY xeroxed mini-books.

Gregory lives with four cats, his brilliant daughter, & with his muse & wife, a chef, engineer, & advocate for sexual assault survivors.

Gregory can be found live at sci-fi and fetish conventions, Evil Grin Poetry Series, Pennsic, or at Dark Odyssey events.

COLLECTIONS

Gregory works have been collected in:

The Department of Constructed Languages
Collection of the Austrian National Library.
The Carter/Johnson Leather Library and
Collection.
The Leather Archives & Museum.
The Museum of Sex, NY.
The Museum of Menstruation online.